SPECIAL OFFERS FOR
LITTLE MISS RE

In every Mr Men and Little Miss book yo[u]
Collect only six tokens and we will send you a super poster of your choice
featuring all your favourite Mr Men or Little Miss friends.

And for the first 1,000 readers we hear from, we will send you a
Mr Men activity pad* and a bookmark* as well – absolutely free!

Return this page with six tokens from Mr Men and/or Little Miss books to:
Marketing Department, World International Publishing, Egmont House,
PO Box 111, 61 Great Ducie Street, Manchester M60 3BL.

Your name:_____

Collect six of these tokens.
You will find one inside every
Mr Men and Little Miss book
which has this special offer.

Address:_____

_____

_____ Postcode: _____

Signature of parent or guardian: _____

I enclose **six** tokens – please send me a Mr Men poster ☐
I enclose **six** tokens – please send me a Little Miss poster ☐

We may occasionally wish to advise you of other children's books that
we publish. If you would rather we didn't, please tick this box ☐

*while stocks last   (Please note: this offer is limited to a maximum of two posters per household.)

1
TOKEN

Please remove this page carefully

Join the
MR.MEN & little miss
Club

Treat your child to membership of the long-awaited Mr Men & Little Miss Club and see their delight when they receive a personal letter from Mr Happy and Little Miss Giggles, a club badge **with their name on**, and a superb Welcome Pack. And imagine how thrilled they'll be to receive a card from the Mr Men and Little Misses on their birthday and at Christmas!

Take a look at all of the great things in the Welcome Pack, every one of them of superb quality (see box right). If it were on sale in the shops, the Pack alone would cost around £12.00. But a year's membership, including all of the other Club benefits, costs just **£7.99** (plus 70p postage) with a 14 day money-back guarantee if you're not delighted.

To enrol your child please send **your** name, address and telephone number together with **your child's** full name, date of birth and address (including postcode) and a cheque or postal order for £8.69 (payable to Mr Men & Little Miss Club) to: Mr Happy, Happyland (Dept. WI), PO Box 142, Horsham RH13 5FJ. Or call 01403 242727 to pay by credit card.

Please note: We reserve the right to change the terms of this offer (including the contents of the Welcome Pack) at any time but we offer a 14 day no-quibble money-back guarantee. We do not sell directly to children - all communications (except the Welcome Pack) will be via parents/guardians. After 31/12/96 please call to check that the price is still valid. Please allow 28 days for delivery. Promoter: Robell Media Promotions Limited, registered in England number 2852153.

The Welcome Pack:

✔ Membership card
✔ Personalized badge
✔ Club members' cassette with Mr Men stories and songs
✔ Copy of Mr Men magazine
✔ Mr Men sticker book
✔ Tiny Mr Men flock figure
✔ Personal Mr Men notebook
✔ Mr Men bendy pen
✔ Mr Men eraser
✔ Mr Men book mark
✔ Mr Men key ring

Plus:

✔ Birthday card
✔ Christmas card
✔ Exclusive offers
✔ Easy way to order Mr Men & Little Miss merchandise

All for just £7·99! (plus 70p postage)

little Miss Neat

by Roger Hargreaves

WORLD INTERNATIONAL
MANCHESTER

Little Miss Neat was a very tidy person.

Probably the tidiest person in the world.

She lived in Twopin Cottage.

It was called Twopin Cottage because she kept it as neat as two pins!

She just couldn't stand a mess.

Every day she spent all day polishing and dusting and cleaning and making sure that things were in their proper places.

One morning little Miss Neat awoke in her bedroom at Twopin Cottage.

She looked out of her bedroom window.

It had been raining during the night, and there was a puddle in the middle of her garden path.

"Oh", she gasped in horror, and rushed outside with a duster.

She mopped up every drop of puddle, and then she rushed inside and washed the duster, and then she ironed the duster, and then she folded the duster, and then she placed the duster very neatly back in its drawer.

Everything in Twopin Cottage had its proper place!

Now, this story is about the time little Miss Neat went on holiday.

She always went away for one week every summer, and this year was no different.

She spent two weeks packing.

And then she spent a whole day polishing her suitcase.

And then off she set leaving Twopin Cottage all spick and span and neat and tidy.

"Oh I hope it doesn't get too dusty while I'm away," she thought as she closed the door behind her.

But something worse than dusty was going to happen to Twopin Cottage.

Would you like to know what?

Mr Muddle came to tea!

He'd written to Miss Neat to tell her, but, being Mr Muddle, he somehow got into a muddle posting the letter.

Actually, what happened was that when Mr Muddle went to post the letter he had the letter in one hand and a half-eaten sandwich in the other.

And you can guess what happened, can't you?

That's right!

He posted the sandwich!

A posted cheese sandwich!

"It'll be nice seeing Miss Neat again,"
he chuckled to himself as he walked home.

"This sandwich is a bit chewy," he thought.

It was the day after Miss Neat left that Mr Muddle arrived.

He walked up the garden path of Twopin Cottage, and knocked at the door.

No reply!

"Goodbye!" he shouted.

It should have been "Hello!" but he isn't called Mr Muddle for nothing.

"Nobody home?" he called.

He pushed open the door.

"Oh dear," he thought as he looked around.

"Nobody home!"

"Never mind," he thought. "I'll make myself a cup of tea and wait for Miss Neat."

So he went into the kitchen of Twopin Cottage, made himself a cup of tea, and waited.

And waited.

And waited.

And waited.

And went home.

Little Miss Neat stepped out of the taxi outside Twopin Cottage.

"That was a lovely holiday," she said, paying the taxi driver. "But it's nice to be home."

She walked up the garden path, and went in through the door.

"Not too dusty," she said to herself looking around.

"I think I'll make myself a nice cup of tea before I start unpacking."

But, making tea after a Mr Muddle visit isn't quite as easy as it sounds.

Little Miss Neat eventually found the teapot.

Not in its proper place.

In the refrigerator!

And she eventually found the milk.

Not in its proper place.

In the teapot!

And the tea.

In the sugar bowl!

And the sugar.

In the milk jug!

And a cup.

In the oven!

And a saucer.

In the breadbin!

But, could she find a teaspoon?

She could not!

The telephone rang.

Little Miss Neat picked it up.

"Hello," she said.

At the other end of the line Mr Muddle suddenly realised he was holding the telephone the wrong way round.

He turned it the right way round.

"Goodbye," he said.

"Who's that?" asked Miss Neat.

"It's you," replied Mr Muddle.

Miss Neat thought.

"It's Mr Muddle, isn't it?" she guessed.

"Yes", replied Mr Muddle, getting it right for once.

"And you paid me a visit while I was away on holiday, didn't you?" she guessed again.

"Yes", replied Mr Muddle, getting it right for twice.

"Can I come and see you now you're back?"

"I suppose so", sighed Miss Neat.

"Goodbye!"

"Hello!" said Mr Muddle.

And put the 'phone down.

Little Miss Neat sighed a heavy sigh, and sat down in the armchair next to the telephone.

Ouch!!

She looked underneath the cushion.

There were all her teaspoons.

And knives!

And forks!

I don't think little Miss Neat will be taking a holiday next year.

Do you?